Dulteer
& the
Jekon

Introduction

"If no man has enough bravery in his heart, enough rage in his veins to do to beast what beast do, enough fire in there

Nivenity to fight these Jekons that torment us, that feed on our flesh but mainly kill us for sport leaving us to rot on there swords, if no man will fight, then I a boy of only 14 years will fight, and if I die I will look upon the great lord Nag in shame for the elder men of my people that they

would rather die
cowards then join me
in battle, but if I shall
live I will forgive your
fear but may my
victory be a lesson
that as long as
Nazeerah is in your
heart you cannot lose,
for our Nag is a Nag
of victory and a Nag
of war"

Episode 1
"War or Servitude"

It was raining when they found me, I guess I got lost in the woods, trees as far as the eye can see, and almost tall enough to reach the sky, so much panic on their faces, boy I really must have had everyone worried. If only things were that simple, instead of blood dripping from bodies skewered on Jekon spears, scattered around what was my village, yet now looked more like a forest of death, I don't know how I survived but I knew why, someone needed to remember, my village, my people, someone needed to feel how I felt so they could rest in peace knowing how much they meant to someone, most of all, someone would need to take revenge. I was seven when my village was destroyed by Jekon kounts, they rampaged, eating the flesh of my people

and drinking their
blood, and who they
didn't eat they
tortured for their
enjoyment and
decorated their
swords and spears
with their bodies,
when they were done,
when their bellies
were full and they
became bored of our
suffering, they just,
left. I was too young

to know what to do, or where to go, so I just laid in the middle of that hellish forest until I was found by a xleva seller leading a small group of captives through my village towards the krodaminion of Gusteero babel. Born so close to a krodaminion I knew a bit about how these so

called civilizations
worked, although my
people were against
them, whisper led to
gossip which gave
way to xkripture,
thats what my mother
always used to say,
since the beginning of
time people have used
whispers to pass on
information in secret,
gossip became that
collective information,

however all gossip has a source, which led to people with differences in opinions being tracked down and punished or killed, thus xkripture was born, coded messages left in writing and even drawings, people learned how to say things without saying a word, how to pass messages without getting caught, that is how my ancestors survived Egyah all those years ago, how the Negarza race passes down information. Krodaminions are dominions ruled over by Krowlocks, and Krowlock is the highest title a leader can receive, and

where there is a
Krowlock there will
always be kounts.
That meant me
encountering this
xleva seller was a
blessing in disguise, a
kount is an elite
warrior, even in the
world of kounts there
is a hierarchy
however a kount of
the lowest rank is
equal to ten high level

warriors. I needed to become a kount, I needed skill, and power, for my people, for my family, for our revenge.

Xleva seller; "what the hell happened here kid?"

Dulteer; "a mistake"

Xleva seller; "a
mistake, ha ha ha,
you got dam right kid,
any group of people
foolish enough to not
run at the first sight of
a Jekon has truly
made a very big
mistake"

Dulteer; "The mistake wasn't ours, the mistake was theirs, because they left me alive, and I will be the death of Jekons"

The look in the xleva sellers eyes, confusion, disbelief,

and fear, my words
were bold but true, I
knew why the great
lord Nag cursed me to
be the only survivor
from my village, it
was my obligation to
be something Jekons
fear, a scary story they
tell their children
about, and a monster
that comes to their
villages to play.

Xleva seller; "well, I guess I won't even be needing chains for you now will I ?"

As the xleva seller marched on with his captives I began to follow behind them, our destination, Babel city. The journey was rough, only ten miles outside my village and already the xleva seller needed a break, and he was on horseback, he was a foolish man, yet I could tell he was capable in battle, as for his captives, most seemed frail, but two seemed physical strong, it wouldn't be enough, not in these woods, these woods where the xleva seller wanted to make camp, these woods, that my village knew belong to Vermaya.

Dulteer; "we can't make camp here, we should continue onward"

Xleva seller; "kid, you might have been walking with us a short while, but we have journeyed over forty miles and we still have around twenty to go"

Dulteer; "you don't get it…"

Xleva seller; "no you don't get it, just sit down and shut up before I cut out your tongue"

Dulteer; "my tongue? You can have it, I don't need to talk to accomplish my goal, I just need to live long enough to become a kount"

Xleva seller; "ha ha ha, kid you really crack me up, thats the only reason I'm tolerating you, but you'll be lucky to be a field hand where your going, most people who buy child xleva like to use them in worse ways, you could end up being some degenerates sex xleva"

Dulteer; "now who's telling jokes, sex xleva? Nazeerahs wrath burns within me, you tolerate me? No I tolerate you, because you can take me where I need to go and you provide the

sacrifice needed to
make it there"

Xleva seller;
"sacrifice?"

Dulteer; "you have
twelve xleva,
including you thats
thirteen sacrifices, but
who knows if thats

enough, thats why we need to leave"

Explaining things was useless, besides it was to late, we were already in the clutches of a Vermaya. She was clearly both experienced and powerful because she chose to attack head on, no trickery, which is what you could expect from lesser vermaya. It was swift, how quickly the scent of blood filled the air, three died before we knew she was there, before they even knew they were dead, they stood there in their chains, disemboweled yet we never heard a sound or even caught a glimpse of her. The xleva seller grabbed his sword and got into a fighting stance instinctively but his face told a tale of fear, his voice cracked as he spoke.

Xleva seller; "my name is Ochmood Jibar, face me demon

and I will take your head"

She crawled out from the shadows, her skin was grey and lacerated, she looked like she had been killed violently, her jaw was broken, hanging there from her face, eyes as blue as the sky, she probably was beautiful once, but all that was left was a tool for evil, her hands and feet were jet black, a sign of a vermaya, she gave off a strange sour smell, that was so strong it eclipsed the scent of fresh blood in the air. She crawled over to

us, slowly, twistedlike,
brokenlike, it was as if
her bones were
braking and repairing
themselves over and
over as she moved
towards us, this was
her true form, no
tricks, no veil, and
then she screamed, so
loud we couldn't hear
it, but we felt it, it was
heavy, like being
submerged deep

within the ocean, we
couldn't move, we
couldn't breathe, it
took everything just to
continue to think, we
were ensnared in her
web of silence.

Ochmood Jibar;
"shut it you whore"

Vermaya; "whore?
Its been awhile since
I've went by that

name, or was that a
title? Or maybe a
nickname? No matter
you'll be dead soon"

   Within an instant
she constructed a veil,
an illusion we were
now trapped in, the
sun was out even
though it was night,
the grass was lush and
green even though we

were just trekking through mud, the tress that were once old willows were now cherry blossoms, and the vermaya who was once horrid and ragged, was now a vision of beauty. Why she felt the need to do this was lost on me, maybe it was just to showoff, or maybe it was mercy, the warmth of this false sun was comforting, there was a cool breeze that was relaxing, I could see on the faces of Ochmoods captives that they had made peace with their coming deaths. Suddenly I couldn't breathe, my neck felt like it was gonna tear, my lungs struggled for air, and my chest felt like it was gonna burst, slowly the veil began to vanish, and I could see the vermaya on top of me, now back in her true form, her hand gripped around my neck, her breath smelled like death, blood dripped from her mouth onto my face, as I tried to look away I saw the

carnage she made of
Ochmood and his
captives, like cattle,
they were gutted,
hollowed out, and
skinned, their bodies
were a sight no one
should ever see, yet all
I could think, was
how could she be this
strong, how much
speed would it take to
do what she did, or
maybe it wasn't

speed, maybe she merely altered my perception of time, I needed power like hers, I needed to live, and yet I was about to die. My throat was burning, and I began to lose consciousness, and then there was a howl, a howl that felt like it shook the entire forest, and suddenly I could breathe, her grip loosened up just enough for air to creep into my lungs, when the howl stopped the forest stopped shaking, but not her, the vermaya was still shaking, she was nervous, she was afraid. What could strike fear in a creature this powerful? The scent of ash and charcoal was in the air, and growling was coming from the distance, glowing eyes of fire contrasted against the darkness of the forest, what was this beast? As if her nail were a blade she slid her finger across my face, from my right cheek, over the bridge of my nose and to my left, it was so quick I didn't feel a thing, blood sprayed out like a mist, and with a finger she wiped some off my face and tasted it, then she stood up and began to walk away. My thoughts raced, I was so confused, I had to know, I needed to know, why wouldn't she just kill me, why was I being left alive for the second time, was I just not worth killing? Was this just a sick joke?

Dulteer; "where the hell are you going?"

Vermaya; "i'm done here, so I'm going to rest"

Dulteer; "aren't you going to kill me?"

Vermaya; "no, it seems that wouldn't be a very smart option, and I haven't lived this long making foolish decisions"

Dulteer; "but why?
Why not just kill me?"

Vermaya; "don't get
me wrong, I would
love to kill you, in fact
your blood is
especially delectable,
but if I were to kill
you I would have to

fight that wolf hiding
in the darkness"

I didn't understand
what she meant at
first, and then I
remembered the
howling and the eyes,
I turned to look
behind me and there

were those glowing eyes of flame, they stayed fixed on me.

Dulteer; "what the hell is that thing?"

Vermaya; "Wardamor, you

should know that, those wolves were cursed by your great lord Nag"

She was right, I did know that, although I never seen one, there was a legend about a Negarza boy who coward while bandits raped and killed his sister only their small dog trying to intervene, this enraged Nazeerah who then cursed the boy for his cowardice, since the dog had more bravery than the boy, Nazeerah cursed the boy by transforming him into a wolf, and since he didn't stand up against the evils of men, he would spend the rest of his life hunting the evils of the world, this curse was then past down through his bloodline.

Dulteer; "so this creature lurking behind me?"

Vermaya; "yeah, one of your ancestors, maybe even a distant

relative, it seems he rather protect you than fight me, but if you were dead I know he wouldn't hold back"

Dulteer; "and so…"
Vermaya; "so you're free to go, after all you are still seeking vengeance right?"

She smiled then vanished, I stood there frozen, no longer afraid, just upset, I was so weak, I almost died, how could I ever hope to face off against a Jekon when I was helpless against a vermaya, these creatures, these monsters were on a whole different level. I stood there for hours, the eyes watching me the whole time, when they finally vanished I knew it was because the vermaya had been long gone, so I continued to head to Babel city. Twenty miles, no food or water, cold and tired, I walked until I reached the edge of the city. I most likely

collapsed from
exhaustion because I
don't remember
entering the city,
when I woke up I was
in front of a fire place
on the floor of
someones shack, there
was a bandage
around my face, and I
could smell food
cooking, I was
starving, I couldn't
remember the last

time I ate, the shack
was pretty big from
what I could deduce,
I was near the fire
place in what seemed
to be a living room,
yet the scent of food
was in the distance,
and there was no bed
in the living room
which meant there
must have been at
least one bedroom,
this led me to the

conclusion this person had a decent amount of money, my family was a family of eight, six kids and my mother and father, we lived in a one room shack, cooked, showered and used the bathroom outside, I needed to figure out where I was and who I was with, because what looks like a

blessing could always
be a curse in disguise.

Dulteer; "hello?
Where am I ?"

???; "so your awake
out there"

The voice was stern, clearly a male voice, by the tone he seemed imposing.

Dulteer; "my name is Dulteer, and yours?"

???; "Dulteer? Thats a good name, my name is Dorn"

Dulteer; "where are we?"

Dorn; "isn't it obvious? This is Babel city"

Dulteer; "so then, I made it here?"

Dorn; "barely, if it weren't for me you'd be dead"

Dulteer; "ha ha ha, yeah, I guess that

vermaya did have me in a bind"

He was right, things were more obvious then he knew, at first the fire distracted me, but that distinct scent of ash and charcoal was unmistakable, Dorn was a Wardamor, and the chances of him being a different one from the one in the woods would be slim to none.

Dorn; "so you figured it out"

Dulteer; "why did you save me?"

After I asked him
why he saved me, he
came from the
kitchen into the living
room, he was a
towering bronze
statue of a man,
covered in scars, and
wearing garments
made of bear skins, he
looked like how I
wanted to look, like
how a man who could

slay a Jekon would look.

Dorn; "I saved you because your Negarza"

Dulteer; "I figured as much"

Dorn; "maybe, or maybe its more

complicated than you think. As a Wardamor my bloodline comes from the Negarza, however, centuries separate our two bloodlines to the point I feel no kinship to you"

Dulteer; "then why save me?"

Dorn; "because we both are children of Nazeerah, and his wrath burns bright in your eyes, I know your survival will mean glory for our great lord Nag, so for me to deny him that would be blasphemous"

Dulteer; "my village…"

Dorn; "there's no need to explain, the scent of death is all over you, and vengeance is painted all over your face"

Dulteer; "…"

Dorn; "so, whats your plan?"

Dulteer; "to become a kount, then I'm going to hunt down and kill as many Jekon as possible"

Dorn; "sounds like a plan, a very stupid plan, ha ha ha"

Dulteer; "well it's the only plan I have"

Dorn; "just get some rest kid, you're gonna need it"

The earth shook, screams of women and children were coming from every direction, I woke up to this, my fathers and older brothers grabbing their spears and rushing out the shack, my mom holding my sisters while they cried, what was happening? I stood up, and I was outside, my home was swept away like leaves in the wind, my mother and sisters blown away by the force, as I looked around I realized my village was gone, what was once a village of homes, schools, and stores, was now a pile of burning rubble and dead bodies, I couldn't move, I couldn't speak, I couldn't even think, I watched those who were still alive fighting in their hearts, yet only dying in reality, there was no fight to be had, these creatures were larger than trees, by simply moving they were causing devastation, what the heck was I supposed to do?

Dorn; "kid, wake up, Dulteer"

Dulteer; "dad?"

Dorn; "you're having a nightmare, get yourself together"

A nightmare? No, it was just a memory, a memory that made the thought of ever sleeping or even closing my eyes feel like a nightmare. I was a coward, I survived by just standing still, how could I become a kount? How could I ever hope to be able to avenge my village?

Dorn; "thinking about your weakness want make you any stronger"

Dulteer; "don't tell me Wardamor can read minds"

Dorn; "ha, no kid, I don't need to be able to read minds to know whats on yours"

Dulteer; "I just need…"

Dorn; "you need to rest, clear your mind, vengeance will only eat you up inside, instead find true drive, true purpose, only then will you find the strength you need"

Dulteer; "true purpose? My entire village being wiped out isn't reason enough?"

Dorn; "only you can answer that, with your actions, not with your words"

Dulteer; "trust me, I will prove it with my actions, just you wait"

Dorn; "is that so? Fine then kid, show me at daybreak, because when the sun rises your training begins"

Dulteer; "you're going to train me?"

Dorn; "and here I thought you were smart, why else would I bring you here?"

My journey was about to began, my mission was clear, my conviction was strong, and I was going to be trained by a monster, to fight against monsters, so that the next time I see a

Jekon, I would be the predator.

To be continued…